PONY DAYS

SHELTIE
and the
SNOW PONY

D0196078

PONY♥DAYS

SHELTIE
and the
SNOW PONY

by Peter Clover

**Cover illustration by
Tristan Elwell**

AN
APPLE
PAPERBACK

SCHOLASTIC INC.

New York Toronto London Auckland Sydney
Mexico City New Delhi Hong Kong Buenos Aires

No part of this publication may be reproduced in whole or in part, or stored in a retrieval system, or transmitted in any form or by any means, electronic, mechanical, photocopying, recording, or otherwise, without written permission of the publisher. For information regarding permission, write to Working Partners Limited, 1 Albion Place, London W6 OQT, United Kingdom.

ISBN 0-439-68887-6

Copyright © 1999 by Working Partners Ltd.
Created by Working Partners Ltd, London W6 OQT.

All rights reserved. Published by Scholastic Inc., 557 Broadway, New York, NY 10012, by arrangement with Working Partners Limited. SHELTIE is a trademark owned by Working Partners Ltd. SCHOLASTIC, APPLE PAPERBACKS, and associated logos are trademarks and/or registered trademarks of Scholastic Inc.

12 11 10 9 8 7 6 5 4 3   4 5 6 7 8 9/0

Printed in the U.S.A.   40

First Scholastic printing, November 2004

For Yvette, Bob, and Bruno

SHELTIE
and the
SNOW PONY

Chapter One

"Brrr!" Emma shivered in her thick jacket. The wind outside was cold enough to freeze her breath.

She stood on the front step and hugged herself to keep warm. Looking up to the sky, she blew white, frosty puffs into the air.

On the ground, everything as far as Emma could see was covered in a dusting of white.

"Jack Frost was busy last night," she said. She pulled up her collar and crunched her way across the grass to the paddock.

Two small ears pricked up expectantly from a wild, unruly mop of frosted forelock. And a pair of gentle brown eyes twinkled brightly as Emma approached. Sheltie, her little Shetland pony, stood waiting with his fuzzy chin resting on the top bar of the wooden gate.

Sheltie could see the apple that Emma was holding. He blew a snort and she scratched him hard between his ears.

"Good morning, boy. Look what I've got for you!"

The apple was soon gone as Sheltie munched happily, pushing his soft nose into Emma's gloved hand, looking for more.

Emma swung her legs over the fence and walked with Sheltie to his field shelter. Sheltie walked close and kept nudging Emma playfully with his muzzle. Emma nudged Sheltie back. But as she leaned into him, Sheltie suddenly skipped sideways and Emma sat down with a bump.

"Ow!" Emma laughed. "You're obviously full of tricks this morning, Sheltie." Then, as Emma sat on the frosty grass, she felt something cold touch her face. It was a snowflake landing gently on her cheek.

"Oh, Sheltie!" said Emma. "It's snowing."

Sheltie looked up to the sky at the fine
white snowflakes floating down from the
clouds. Emma broke the ice on Sheltie's
water trough and fished out the frozen
pieces with her trowel.

"Come on, Sheltie. Breakfast!" Emma scooped the pony mix into the feed manger and watched as Sheltie wolfed it down.

Sheltie liked his food. If Emma wasn't careful, she would have a pony that was as fat as a barrel!

"Your trouble is that you're spoiled rotten," said Emma. "You've got every-thing you could possibly wish for, don't you?"

Sheltie gave Emma a mischievous look, then nuzzled up closely and shut his eyes contentedly.

Emma gave Sheltie a kiss. His thick winter coat smelled of fresh air and snow. And he looked just like a big, cuddly toy.

After filling Sheltie's hayrack, Emma

went back indoors for her own breakfast. The kitchen was warm and cozy, with pine cupboards and bright red gingham curtains. Bacon sizzled on the grill and the smell made Emma's mouth water as she stepped inside, out of the cold.

After breakfast, Mom asked, "What are you going to do today, Emma? Dad's taking me and Joshua shopping in Rilchester. Do you want to come?"

Emma liked going out with Mom and Dad. But she would rather take Sheltie out for a ride in the snowy countryside any day.

"I thought I might take Sheltie out over the fields," said Emma. "To see if it's been snowing up there."

"Poor old Sheltie." Mom laughed. "I bet

he'd much rather stay in his nice, comfortable paddock!"

"No, he wouldn't," said Emma. "Anyway, I'm keeping him fit. Exercise is good for ponies."

Mom didn't dare argue.

"You're right," she said. "When it comes to Sheltie, Emma, you always know best."

Mom, Dad, and Joshua left for Rilchester soon after breakfast. Emma put on an extra sweater under her jacket and wrapped her favorite scarf around her neck. Then she adjusted her riding hat, fixed the strap under her chin, and went out to tack up Sheltie.

The paddock gleamed white beneath its light covering of snow.

Sheltie pranced and snorted, pawing a

hole in the snow with his hoof. The little pony was eager to be off. He loved going out, whatever the weather.

Emma walked Sheltie out into the lane. Then they crossed the snow-covered meadow at a trot as they headed for Bramble Wood and the fields beyond.

The freezing wind made Emma's eyes run and her face turn pink. But Sheltie didn't seem to feel the cold at all. His thick, hairy coat and shaggy mane kept him nice and warm.

Emma crouched low over Sheltie's neck as she rode him faster across the fields. It hadn't been snowing much up there after all. Sheltie's hooves drummed the hard ground.

"We're going to win, Sheltie! We're going

to win!" Emma was pretending that they
were in a race. She was so lost in her game
that she didn't pay attention to where she
was heading.

Sheltie finally slowed down to a walk.

"Where are we, Sheltie?" Emma looked around.

She suddenly realized that they were in the East Meadow. Emma urged Sheltie to follow a path that wound its way through a valley. The valley would lead them back to Barrow Hill and the village of Little Applewood, where Emma lived.

Before long, they were riding in the valley and following a bridle path that suddenly forked off in two directions.

Emma knew that one path led to the village. She wasn't sure where the other path led.

"Come on, Sheltie! Let's go exploring."

Sheltie sniffed at the air. Then he shook out his mane and jangled his reins, eager to follow the new path.

Chapter Two

Emma and Sheltie found themselves in a very narrow, overgrown lane, deep-set between tall hedges and trees that almost met overhead. The hedges and trees were icy and frosted white.

"Oh, look, Sheltie," said Emma. "A snow tunnel."

Halfway down the tunnel, Sheltie's ears pricked up. Emma heard something, too! It was the sound of a pony neighing. And it was coming from somewhere behind the hedge.

Sheltie found a gap and Emma peered through into someone's yard. It wasn't much of a yard, really. More of a dry frozen patch with bushes and bare trees. And there, right in the middle, tethered to one of those trees, was a small brown pony.

The rope that tethered the pony had wound itself around the poor creature's legs. It stood there unable to move.

Emma quickly found a gate hidden in the hedge. Without a second thought, she slid off Sheltie and walked with him up to the back door of the house.

The brown pony looked up with big, sad eyes. Sheltie called to the pony with a soft whicker. He seemed to know that this pony was in trouble.

Emma noticed a nameplate that read LEWIS next to the door knocker. She knocked loudly on the door and waited.

It took a long time before the door opened. But when it did, a nicely dressed woman, whom Emma assumed was Mrs. Lewis, stood on the step,

"Hello," the woman said with a bright,

friendly smile. "Are you selling something?"

Emma was taken aback. "No, I'm not," she said. "It's your pony!"

"My pony?" The woman seemed puzzled.

"Yes, your pony!" said Emma. "He's very tangled up in his rope. His tether is far too long and it's all wound around his legs."

"Oh, no, not again," replied the woman. "The silly thing keeps doing that! Would you give me a hand? I'm hopeless with animals."

Pulling the door closed on the latch behind her, the woman beckoned Emma and Sheltie to follow her into the yard. She held Sheltie's rein while Emma approached the pony. As she untied the cord from the tree, Emma felt a wave of pity pass over her for the poor tethered animal.

The pony watched Emma's every move as she carefully untangled the rope.

As soon as he was free, the pony ambled over to Sheltie and they rubbed noses.

"Oh!" squealed the woman. "What are they doing? They're not going to fight, are they?" She held Sheltie's rein at arm's length.

Emma couldn't help giggling. "They're just saying hello!" she said. "That's how ponies say hi. They rub noses."

"Oh, I can see you're an expert," the woman said, smiling. And she really meant it.

"Well, I do know a lot about ponies," said Emma. She wanted to tell the woman that this pony looked too thin. That the poor thing would freeze without a rug or a shelter. And that there wasn't nearly enough grass for the pony to graze. It needed pony feed and sweet, fresh hay. And water.

But Emma didn't say any of these things. She didn't want to sound rude. So instead she asked, "How old is he?"

"Oh, my!" said the woman. "I've no idea."

"Is he *your* pony?" inquired Emma.

"Well, yes, he is now," she said. "I saw Prince advertised in the newspaper as an abandoned stray and bought him for my daughter. She's away at boarding school at the moment. We live up north, but we often come here for weekends.

"The dealer said that he had been abandoned in a field. He's a rescued pony, you see, and I thought Jessica would love to have him. We thought it would make a nice surprise present for her birthday next week."

Emma listened to this with interest.

"Mind you," the woman continued, "since he was delivered two days ago he's been nothing but trouble. But then I don't know much about ponies."

Emma looked at Prince. She couldn't

imagine him being any trouble at all. The
brown pony nuzzled up to Sheltie as
though he had found a long-lost friend.
Sheltie looked so fat standing next to
him. Sheltie's thick, woolly coat would
keep him warm in the coldest weather.

And his plump belly would never be empty.

Emma wanted to do something to help poor Prince. She wanted Prince to feel loved and wanted, too.

"I hope he's going to be an excellent jumper," said the woman suddenly.

"Does Jessica like jumping?" asked Emma.

"Well, I expect she will once she's learned to ride," said the woman.

A look of surprise swept across Emma's face. Jessica had never even ridden a pony! Suddenly, Emma couldn't keep quiet any longer.

"But what about a stable for Prince when you're not here?" said Emma. "The poor thing will freeze in this weather. He looks so cold already!"

"Oh, don't worry about that, my dear girl," said the woman. "He's going to a stable for winter boarding. He's too much of a handful for me to keep here on my own."

Emma breathed a sigh of relief. At least the pony was going to have a roof over his head and some warm straw for the winter. Maybe this woman wasn't so scatterbrained after all.

"Which stable is going to board him?" asked Emma. "Will it be Crossways?"

"Oh, I haven't decided yet," the woman said vaguely. "I've got to make some inquiries." She looked at her watch. "Well, I must go now. Thank you for your help."

"If you like, I'll shorten his tether for you so he won't get tangled up again," said Emma. "And if you've got an old blanket,

21

I'll show you how to make a rug to keep him warm."

"That's very kind of you," said the woman. "But I don't think we have any old blankets. You can shorten his rope if you like while I have a look!" Then she checked her watch again and hurried back inside, leaving Emma and Sheltie alone with the shivering pony.

Chapter Three

Emma shortened Prince's tether as she said she would, then rubbed at the hard, icy ground with the toe of her boot. She scraped away the frost and said, "Look at that, Sheltie! He's already cropped back the grass to the bare earth. There's nothing here at all for poor Prince to graze on." Then she noticed a laurel tree growing in the yard. "And that laurel's poisonous to ponies," she added. "I'll adjust his tether again, Sheltie, just to make sure Prince can't reach those leaves."

Then she went to say good-bye to the thin, gentle pony.

Mrs. Lewis came back to say that she didn't have any old blankets. Then she rushed off again.

Emma had a plan.

"Don't worry, boy," she said to Prince. "We'll come back this afternoon with a nice warm rug and some good feed."

Prince pushed his soft muzzle into Emma's chest and whickered quietly.

Emma noticed that the old halter he wore had been marked with his name. PRINCE it said, in faded letters.

"Someone must have loved you once," said Emma. She thought hard about what the dealer had said to Mrs. Lewis about

Prince being abandoned. "What kind of
person could possibly have abandoned
you?" Then Emma gave the pony a
big hug.

That afternoon, after lunch, Emma and
Sheltie came back with an old blanket,

some lengths of soft rope, and a bag stuffed with hay and pony feed.

As they rode through the white tunnel, small snowflakes began to fall again. Sheltie let out a tremendous whinny as if he wanted to tell Prince they were coming.

The thin pony answered with a weak snort, and as they came into the yard the poor thing pricked up his ears and tried to greet them with a loud neigh. But he didn't seem to have the strength and just made a sad noise as he blew weakly through his lips.

Emma knocked at the back door and waited, but there was no answer.

"Maybe Mrs. Lewis had gone to a stable to talk about Prince's boarding, Sheltie," said Emma.

Sheltie shook out the snowflakes from his mane and blew a raspberry.

"Was that for her?" Emma grinned.

Sheltie pawed at the hard ground.

"I guess it was," she said.

Emma got busy with the blanket and lengths of rope. Prince stood perfectly still while Emma threw the cover across the pony's bare back. She carefully tied two corners of the blanket across Prince's chest, then used the ropes like girths to secure the makeshift blanket in place.

"There!" said Emma when she was done. "Is that better, Prince?"

The pony seemed grateful and gave a friendly snort.

Next, Emma piled the hay beneath a tree and tipped out the pony mix next to it. Immediately, Prince wolfed down the

feed, then began munching hungrily on
the hay.

Emma and Sheltie stayed with Prince for
half an hour. Then the snow began to fall
heavier than ever.

"We'd better go now," said Emma. She
decided to look up "Lewis" in the phone
book when she got back home, to see if
Prince *had* been booked into a stable.

"People shouldn't have ponies if they can't look after them," said Emma. She hoped that Jessica Lewis would take better care of Prince than her mother did.

The snow continued to fall, and by the time Emma arrived back at her house, thick drifts were already piling up against the hedges. She settled Sheltie into his shelter and went inside to look for Mrs. Lewis's phone number.

There was only one Lewis listed in Little Applewood, and after dinner, Emma called the number several times. But there was no answer.

Mom could see that Emma was worried. Emma had told Mom all about Prince.

"Maybe Mrs. Lewis is visiting friends, Emma," suggested Mom. "Or maybe she's at the stable, getting Prince settled in!"

"I wonder which stable is boarding Prince," said Emma. "Crossways is the nearest."

"Would you like me to give them a call, Emma?" said Mom. "Just to put your mind at rest."

"Yes, please. It's snowing really hard now, and if Prince isn't stabled anywhere, he could freeze to death!"

Mom made several telephone calls. She spoke to Crossways, Castles, and two other stables in the area. But none were winter-boarding a dark brown pony named Prince. And none of them had even spoken to a Mrs. Lewis about such a possibility.

"There *are* more stables, toward Rilchester," said Mom.

"But they're miles away," said Emma. "Why would Mrs. Lewis board Prince at a stable that it takes ages to get to? If Jessica Lewis is going to ride Prince, then she'd want him to be nearby!"

Mom knew that Emma was right.

"Maybe winter-boarding at a stable was too expensive," suggested Mom. "Maybe Mrs. Lewis has tried to find a farmer with an empty barn."

Emma listened. But she had already decided what she was going to do. Whatever arrangements Mrs. Lewis had made, Emma was going to ride over, first thing in the morning, and find out for herself.

Chapter Four

Later that evening, Emma asked Mom if
she could phone Sally. Sally was Emma's
best friend and had a pony named
Minnow. Sally had been away with her
mother for a few days, visiting an aunt, but
she had returned to Little Applewood that
evening.

Emma wanted to tell Sally all about
Prince. She knew without asking that Sally
would want to help.

". . . so I'll meet you in the morning,"
said Emma.

"I'll be there," said Sally. "Nine o'clock."

*

The next morning, after a quick breakfast, Emma tacked up Sheltie and stuffed two bags full with hay. Then she scooped some pony mix into a third bag.

Sheltie watched all this with great interest. His own hayrack was bulging and he had already gobbled up his breakfast. Sheltie cocked his head to one side.

"I bet you're wondering who this is for, aren't you, Sheltie?" said Emma. "Well, it's for Prince. If he's still at the Lewises' house, then he'll be grateful for a good feed."

Sheltie blew frosty puffs from his nostrils. The morning was cold and crisp. And there were at least five inches of snow on the ground.

Sheltie enjoyed the snow. He liked trampling through the deeper white drifts and lifting his hooves high. His long tail brushed the snowy lane and at times his fat belly dipped into soft, snowy mounds.

Emma rode carefully, keeping Sheltie in the center of the road. She didn't want him stumbling into any hidden dips or holes.

Emma and Sheltie looked up at all the rooftops. They were completely covered with snow. It looked like a topping of whipped cream.

"Isn't it lovely, Sheltie?" said Emma. She leaned forward and patted the little pony's neck. And as she did so, a snowball flew past her head.

"Who threw that?" Emma sat upright in the saddle. She couldn't see anyone. A second snowball hit Sheltie smack on the forelock, right on top of his head.

Sheltie harrumphed playfully, then

blew a raspberry and looked across toward a large, white, snow-covered bush.

Emma followed Sheltie's lead and steered him closer for a better look.

"It's Sally," whispered Emma. "Look, Sheltie. There's Minnow's tail sticking out."

Sheltie could see his pony friend's tail swishing backward and forward. Sheltie's ears pricked up instantly.

Emma slid out of the saddle and quickly made an enormous snowball. Then she pointed to the other side of the bush and hoped Sheltie would trot around on his own.

Sheltie seemed to understand and did what Emma thought he would. Emma crept around the other way.

Sally was surprised to see Sheltie on his own. But she was even more surprised when a snowball the size of a grapefruit exploded on top of her riding hat.

"Gotcha!" yelled Emma, as she leaped into view from behind.

Sally burst out laughing. Minnow threw back his head and blew a loud snicker. After all, he hadn't expected to be showered with snow. Sheltie added to the fun by butting Emma with his nose, sending her flying headlong into the snow-covered bush.

"That'll teach you to sneak up on people!" Sally smiled, brushing snow from her shoulders.

Emma grinned. It was great having a friend like Sally.

Sheltie and Minnow walked along side by side. They trundled through the snow, kicking up their heels as more flurries slowly drifted down from the sky. Sheltie gave a snort as they approached the snow tunnel that led to the Lewises' house.

Before they reached the gate in the long hedge, Sheltie seemed worried. He stopped, flicked up his ears, and sniffed at the icy breeze.

"What is it, boy?" said Emma. "What's the matter?"

Emma's little Shetland pony called out with a whinny. It was almost as if he was trying to tell Emma that something was very wrong.

Sheltie and Minnow stopped at the wooden gate and stood at attention, side by side. Sheltie poked his head over the top bar and blew an urgent snort.

Emma and Sally gasped aloud, then looked on in horror. There was a brown heap lying on the snow-covered ground. It was Prince!

Emma quickly slipped down from the saddle and ran straight into the yard with Sheltie trotting after her. Sally tethered

Minnow loosely to a shrub and rushed
to help.

"Knock on the door," said Emma. "See if
Mrs. Lewis is in."

Sally knocked and knocked, but there
was no reply.

The snow was falling heavier now
and Emma was already on her knees

brushing snowflakes off Prince's head.
Sheltie softly nuzzled the brown pony's
forelock.

Prince's eyes flickered, and he paddled
feebly with his forelegs. Emma felt tears
filling her eyes. The poor pony didn't
have the strength to get himself up.

"Oh, Emma!" croaked Sally. "He looks
terrible. What should we do?"

"We've got to get him warm," said
Emma. "And quickly." She tipped out
one of the hay-filled bags and grabbed
two big fistfuls.

"Come on, Sally. We'll rub him warm."
She felt Prince's legs. They were ice cold.
"Legs first!"

The two girls used the pads of hay to
rub the pony's legs. Emma worked her

way up to his shoulder, rubbing hard,
trying to make the pony warm. Sally
rubbed, too, and worked her way down
his back.

Prince stirred and tried to lift his
head. But he was far too weak. The snow
continued to fall, but luckily the blanket
that Emma had tied was still in place.
It had slipped a little, though, so Emma
pulled at it to cover Prince's bare shoulder.
Then she stuffed some hay underneath.

"I think it's working," said Emma.
"Keep rubbing, Sally!"

"But we can't stay here all morning,"
said Sally. "Shouldn't one of us go for help
before this snow gets worse?"

While Emma was thinking what to do,
Sheltie laid himself down next to Prince

and gently pressed his warm back against the thin pony's back.

"Oh, look," said Sally. "Sheltie's trying to help."

"You keep rubbing, Sally. I'll take Sheltie's saddle off so he can get closer."

Prince opened his eyes and blew the softest, quietest whicker that Emma and Sally had ever heard.

"He's hardly got any strength at all," said Sally.

"But I think he's getting warmer," said Emma. "I'll stay here with Sheltie. You take Minnow and go knock on one of the houses farther up the road. Tell them what's happened and ask them to call Dr. Thorne, the vet. Tell them it's urgent!"

Sally jumped up and rushed back

toward Minnow. She cleared his saddle
with the sleeve of her jacket.

"Come on, boy. This is a real emergency."
Sally quickly mounted and took Minnow
up the road as fast as she could.

Chapter Five

Emma tried to tempt Prince with a
handful of pony mix, but he was too weak
even to eat.

"Don't die, Prince. Please don't die,"
whispered Emma. "Try to hang on just a
little longer. Sally will bring help and
everything will be all right, you'll see!
Just hang on. Please!"

Emma wrapped her arms around the
pony's neck and continued rubbing until

her shoulders ached. Sheltie's thick winter coat felt warm against Prince's back. Emma was glad Sheltie was there. He kept making soft noises that seemed to reassure the sick pony.

Emma snuggled down with the two ponies and tried to keep warm herself. The air had turned icy cold and the sky was a grubby white. It looked as if there was still a lot of snow to fall.

Snowflakes fell and settled on them as they lay there, waiting. Emma kept brushing them off. But no sooner had she cleared the snow than a fresh covering laid itself upon them.

Emma shivered. She was beginning to feel the cold herself.

Emma talked to Prince. He seemed to be listening and twitched his ears.

"Don't worry, Prince. Sally will be here soon with help." But Emma was thinking, *What's happened to her? Why is it taking so long?* She stroked both ponies' faces and Sheltie whickered gently. He seemed to be saying, *I'm still here. I'll keep you warm.*

Emma was wondering whether she should leave Prince for a while and take Sheltie to look for Sally and Minnow. She was beginning to think that something had happened to them, when she heard the sound of car tires crunching snow outside in the road on the other side of the hedge. Then she heard Sally's voice calling, "Emma! Emma! We're here!"

Sally rushed into the yard. "This is Mr. Baker from the last house up the road. No one else along the way was in." Sally breathed heavily. "I had to go right to the end and it took forever. Mrs. Baker has called the vet and Mr. Baker has come to help. He knows all about ponies."

Mr. Baker had brought a comforter from his spare bedroom and some nice thick blankets. He wrapped one around Emma, then threw the comforter and two other blankets across Prince.

Sheltie rolled up onto his feet and shook the snow from his thick, shaggy coat. Mr. Baker began rubbing Prince all over just like Emma and Sally had, to help warm him up.

Sheltie tossed his head and shook more snow from his mane. Then he looked toward the hedge as he heard the sound of another vehicle pulling up outside in the road.

Emma rushed to see who it was. It was
Dr. Thorne, the vet, driving a horse trailer.

The snow continued to fall as Dr.
Thorne came through the gate and joined
them.

The vet bent over Prince with a stethoscope, shaking his head. Prince didn't move.

"Is he dead?" asked Emma nervously.

"No," said Dr. Thorne. "But he's in bad shape. It's good you came along when you did." He rooted around in his bag and gave Prince an injection.

Just then, Mrs. Baker came running into the yard. She had stayed behind to make sure the vet was coming, and now hurried to help them.

"Oh, the Lewises' poor pony. Mrs. Lewis told my neighbor that their daughter had had an accident at school and she had to drop everything and drive up north first thing this morning. She was still desperate to find Prince a winter stable, but hadn't had time."

"That's no excuse," said Dr. Thorne. "What this pony needs now is warmth and tender loving care."

Mrs. Lewis had seemed to have forgotten all about getting Prince into a stable and had hurried off in a panic to be with her daughter.

"The dealer should never have let Mrs. Lewis have Prince without first telling her how to care for him," said Dr. Thorne. "Let's see if we can get him onto his feet, then once in the trailer we can decide what to do with him."

"He can come and stay with us," said Emma. "There's plenty of room in Sheltie's field shelter."

Dr. Thorne called Emma's dad on his cell phone and made sure it would be OK.

They managed to get Prince onto his feet, but he was very weak and wobbly.

Sheltie nuzzled up to the pony and blew encouraging snorts. It was almost as though Sheltie was trying to get Prince to follow him.

Whatever Sheltie's snorts meant, Prince understood. And with everyone helping, the pony managed to walk slowly up the ramp and into the waiting trailer. Mr. Baker said he would drive while the vet stayed in the back with Prince.

The snow was very thick on the road, and the going was hard and slow. Emma and Sally followed behind the trailer on Sheltie and Minnow.

When they reached Sally's neighborhood, Emma said good-bye and followed the

trailer alone. She walked Sheltie in the
deep ruts that the tires made in the snow.

Once outside Emma's house, Emma
rode Sheltie right up through the yard to
the kitchen and called out for Mom and
Dad to come help.

Chapter Six

While Dr. Thorne tended to Prince in
the trailer and gave him another injection,
Emma told her parents everything that
had happened. She untacked Sheltie,
then helped Dad lay a thick bedding
of straw across the floor of the field
shelter.

Mom came out with an extra-thick
blanket as Prince settled down on the soft
bed and gave a long sigh. Mom covered

him with the warm blanket and knelt down to stroke his tired face.

"There, there, Prince," she said. "We'll look after you and make you better. You poor pony."

Dad hung up a heat lamp and connected it to his spare car battery. Then he watched as Sheltie lay down again next to Prince and snuggled up close to give the pony some extra warmth.

"You'll need to feed him bran mashes for a few days until he gets his strength back," said the vet. "Little and often. But it's nice and cozy in here out of the snow. What he needs more than anything is warmth and company. And I think Sheltie is going to see to that, aren't you, boy?"

Sheltie raised his head and blew a soft snort.

Emma knew Sheltie would do every-thing he could to help Prince. Even if it meant lying as close as possible to him through the night.

After the vet left to drive Mr. Baker home, Dad went to chop some more logs for the fire and Mom went back to the house to check on Joshua, who was taking a nap.

Emma sat with the two ponies for a while, to make sure Prince was settled in. She stroked the pony's neck and smiled. "He already feels a lot warmer, Sheltie," she said.

Prince opened his eyes and looked around him. He seemed happy to be somewhere safe and warm.

Later, Emma helped Mom to prepare a bran mash for Prince, and hand-fed him

as he lay on his bed of straw. The starved
pony took the feed hungrily.

"Don't give him too much, Emma. Little
and often was what the vet said." Mom
smiled.

Emma glanced up. "He is going to be all
right, isn't he?" she asked.

"I think he will be," said Mom. "Dr. Thorne said he would stop by tomorrow to check on Prince's progress. And the injections seem to be helping."

It was true. Prince already seemed like a happier pony. And his coat felt warm under Emma's hand.

The next morning, Emma woke up bright and early. The snow had stopped falling and the sky was now clear and blue. Birds sang in the bare branches of the trees. And as Emma rubbed the windowpane and cleared a peephole in the frosty glass, she saw a wonderful sight out in the paddock.

Everything as far as she could see was covered in a bright white blanket of snow.

And there, waiting by the paddock gate, were Sheltie and Prince. The pony had pulled himself to his feet to take a look at the outside world and had followed Sheltie over to the fence. He still looked wobbly on his legs. But he was standing on his own and looked interested in everything around him.

Emma hurried downstairs to make a breakfast mash for Prince before school. She filled the bowl carefully and carried it out to the paddock.

"Breakfast time," called Emma.

Sheltie seemed to know that the bowl of mash wasn't for him and waited patiently for his own breakfast while Emma fed Prince first.

"That's a good boy, Sheltie," said Emma. "You know Prince is hungry, don't you?"

Sheltie nuzzled Prince with his soft muzzle and watched him eat. And he didn't try to steal one mouthful. Sheltie waited until Prince had finished and then Sheltie stuck his nose in and licked the bowl clean.

"It's your turn now, Sheltie." Emma laughed as she scooped pony mix into the feed manger.

Sheltie wolfed down most of it, then stepped back to offer Prince some of his own breakfast.

The brown pony looked at the mix in the manger, then whickered softly and took the last few pieces.

"You can have some more of that later, Prince," said Emma. "But we don't want to give you too much just yet."

Prince pushed his nose into Emma's

hand and licked her palm. He was such a
sweet pony.

Over the next few days, Prince made a
remarkable recovery.

"He's a tough fella," said Dr. Thorne
when he came on his visits. "And really
quite a healthy pony. At first I was
worried that he might have caught
pneumonia. But it was just the cold
that had gotten to him. He's going to
be fine!"

Sheltie nudged the vet with his head
and blew a cheeky raspberry.

"Prince doesn't have a nice thick
winter coat like you, Sheltie," he added.
"So keeping him out of the weather was
the best cure — that and proper feeding.
This sort of thing happens sometimes

when people take on animals without
thinking it through first."

The paddock was still covered with
snow, so there was no grass to graze on.
But there was plenty of hay and as much
pony mix as Prince needed. Emma fed him
chopped carrots and apples, too. She
liked having two ponies to look after.

Every day, Prince grew stronger. His ears weren't so floppy and his eyes became bright and lively. He even enjoyed a romp or two with Sheltie, chasing around the paddock in games of "catch me if you can" and tag.

It was still freezing cold outside. But Mom had borrowed a real pony rug, and Prince felt nice and warm. And at night, he and Sheltie slept in the field shelter.

On Saturday when the vet called, he had some news from Mrs. Lewis. Mrs. Baker had managed to contact her and had told her all about Prince and what had happened.

"Mrs. Lewis will be staying with her daughter in their other house," said Dr. Thorne.

"Is Jessica all right?" asked Emma.

"Jessica's fine, but apparently they won't be coming back down for weeks. Mrs. Lewis is very worried about Prince, though, and now thinks that having a weekend pony doesn't seem like such a good idea after all. She doesn't think she will be able to look after Prince properly."

"So it looks as though we have an orphan on our hands," said Mom.

Dr. Thorne raised his eyebrows. "Mrs. Lewis asked if you wouldn't mind looking after him and try to find Prince a nice home with someone who could care for him properly. She feels terrible that Prince got so ill. Her intentions were good but she just didn't think."

Mom and Dad discussed the problem.

"Well, Mrs. Lewis has offered to pay all expenses and vet bills, so I suppose Prince will be no trouble," said Mom.

"And there's plenty of room in Sheltie's paddock," added Emma brightly.

Sheltie blew a loud snort. He seemed to like the idea, too! Having a live-in friend was great fun for the little Shetland pony.

"Maybe the riding school will take him on," suggested Dad. "He's a bright pony and very friendly."

"That *would* be best for Prince," said Mom. "After all, he's going to need execise. And you have your hands more than full with Sheltie, Emma."

Emma knew that Mom was right.

"But we won't do anything just yet," said Dad. "We'll get him as fit as a fiddle first. Then we'll decide."

Emma felt happier about that. At least she could look after Prince until then. And if he *did* go to the riding school, she knew he would be well taken care of.

Chapter Seven

Two weeks passed and the snow disappeared as quickly as it had come. The paddock was green again with plenty of grass for the two ponies to graze.

Prince filled out nicely and looked like a completely different pony. He followed Sheltie everywhere and wouldn't leave his little friend's side.

When Emma went out riding, she took Prince along on a lead rein. And he was happy to trot alongside and go wherever Sheltie went.

One Saturday, Emma and Sheltie were riding with Sally and Minnow. They took Prince with them, and as it was such a beautiful sunny morning, they decided to go for a long ride across the field.

Emma liked riding on the field. She loved the way it stretched out as far as they could see. And there were still parts that she and Sally hadn't explored fully.

As they rode side by side, chatting happily, they both noticed a slight change in Prince. The pony was still happy to walk on the lead rein, but he seemed to become more frisky and lightened his step the farther they went on the field. He took deep breaths of cool, fresh crisp air and blew out long plumes of steam from his nostrils. Then his ears pricked up to attention and he tossed his head, looking around at his surroundings.

"Prince seems to be really enjoying himself," said Sally.

"I've never seen him look so happy." Emma smiled.

Sheltie noticed, too, and blew funny pony snorts as though he were talking to his friend.

When they came to a part of the field where neither Emma nor Sally had been before, Prince started pulling forward and decided to take the lead.

"Do you get the feeling that Prince knows where he is?" asked Sally.

"It's almost as though he recognizes this place," agreed Emma. Then before either of them could say any more, Prince broke into a gentle trot.

Sheltie and Minnow quickened their pace and trotted, too.

"I think Prince knows exactly where he is," said Emma. "Come on, Sally. Let's see where he wants to go. I'm sure he wants to take us somewhere!"

Emma let the lead rein out to its full length and Prince rolled into a slow canter.

Sheltie's little legs managed to keep up and Minnow's stride kept Sally alongside.

Six pairs of hooves drummed the hard ground as the posse of three ponies and two riders covered the new stretch of field.

They rode on for a few minutes. Then, without any warning, Prince turned to his right and began following a rough cart track. The track led toward a distant house half hidden by a grove of trees.

Prince rushed up to the wall and stood with his head over a gate looking into a little yard.

"Who could possibly live here?" said Sally.

"I have no idea," answered Emma. "But I think Prince knows."

Prince threw up his head and whinnied loudly. Emma had never heard him make such a loud noise before. Then Sheltie joined in and finally Minnow as well. Between them, the three ponies were making a terrible din.

Emma and Sally started to giggle. They

both thought it was really funny and
hoped that whoever lived there didn't
mind.

Suddenly, the door swung open and a
gray-haired woman stepped out. Emma
and Sally stopped laughing at once. The
woman's face looked very stern. Then
she saw Prince and her face lit up with a
huge smile.

"Prince! Is that you? My darling boy!" Her voice sounded shaky and tired.

Prince blew another series of soft snorts.

"It *is* you! Oh, my darling boy, wherever have you been? Oh, what smart girls to find my darling Prince!"

Emma and Sally exchanged glances. This lady was obviously Prince's original owner. Prince knew her immediately and pushed his velvety muzzle into her outstretched hand. Then the woman gave Prince's neck a big hug and her eyes turned watery with tears.

It was such a lovely scene. But all Emma could think about was, how did Prince end up in Mrs. Lewis's yard?

Surely this kind person wouldn't have abandoned Prince. She obviously loved him to pieces.

Emma could tell by Sally's face that she was thinking the same thing.

The woman opened the gate and let them all into the small yard. She said her name was Mrs. Warner.

Prince immediately nuzzled up as close as he could to his long-lost owner.

"Come inside. I'll make some nice hot cocoa. Then we can sit by the fire and you

can tell me where you found my darling Prince."

Emma and Sally left Sheltie, Prince, and Minnow to graze in the walled yard. There were no flowers or vegetables for the ponies to destroy, and Mrs. Warner seemed quite happy for them to be there.

Sheltie was extra curious and tried to follow Emma into the cottage.

"No!" said Emma. "You wait outside with Prince and Minnow."

"I don't mind," said Mrs. Warner. "There's nothing in here that he can harm."

Emma grinned. She liked this funny old lady. But she still wasn't going to allow Sheltie to come inside. "He's got to learn that he can't just wander into people's houses whenever he feels like it," Emma said.

Sheltie was happy to stand just outside the open door while Mrs. Warner told Prince's story. He stood very quietly in case he was shooed away.

"I'll make the cocoa first," said Mrs. Warner. Then she sat by the fire and began to tell them what had happened.

Chapter Eight

Emma and Sally listened carefully to everything that Mrs. Warner said.

"When my husband died last year, I didn't think I would be able to keep Prince. But Harry loved that pony. And so do I," she added, "with all my heart. So I kept Prince and tried to manage as best I could. He had originally belonged to our grandson, but when the family moved to Australia, we agreed to take care of him.

"After Harry's death, the price of hay got too high and I started letting Prince out onto the field to graze. He seemed safe and always came back. Every night, like clockwork, he'd come trotting through the yard gate and around to his little stable at the back." Mrs. Warner's voice trailed off and she looked down at her slippers.

Emma sipped her cocoa. "What happened then?" she asked.

Mrs. Warner looked up again. "Well, one day he didn't come back. Prince just disappeared and I haven't seen him from then to this day. I tried to find Prince. I walked the field and pinned up signs, but I heard nothing."

Emma guessed what must have happened. "Prince must have wandered farther out on the field than he intended," said Emma, "and been mistaken for a stray. The dealer must have taken Prince and sold him to Mrs. Lewis. She probably thought she was doing him a favor."

Emma told Mrs. Warner all about Mrs. Lewis. The old lady looked very upset when she heard what had happened.

"I expect there was a notice in the newspaper, but I never read the papers these days. Oh, my poor darling Prince," she said. "I would never have abandoned him or turned him out onto the field to fend for himself. There's been a terrible mistake."

Then Emma told Mrs. Warner of Dad's idea about the riding stables.

Mrs. Warner brightened a little when she heard about that.

"Well, I can't really afford to keep him

anymore," she said. "So I guess that if the stables *did* take him on, he would at least be well cared for."

"And you could go and see him whenever you wanted," added Sally.

It seemed like a very good idea and the perfect solution.

Mrs. Warner thought about it for a moment, then said, "If this riding stable is near the field and promises to take care of him, then I suppose it will be the best thing for Prince after all. He used to love being ridden. And he loves children, too."

"Why don't I ask my dad to ask at the stables for you?" suggested Emma. "You can keep him here until we have any news, if you like!"

"Maybe it's best in the long run if you take him with you and arrange it all," said

Mrs. Warner. "He seems happy enough to be with you and you've done an excellent job of taking care of him so far."

Sheltie seemed to agree and gave a loud snort that made Mrs. Warner jump. They had forgotten all about Sheltie for a moment. He had been so quiet, standing there on the doorstep.

They said their good-byes, then Emma and Sally took Prince home.

Dad contacted the riding stable right away and they said they would be very happy to take Prince. They wanted to see him first, but when they heard the whole story, they were almost certain that they could give Prince a good home for life. Someone would come by later that day to take a look at him.

*

The next day, Sunday, Emma and Sheltie delivered Prince to the stable. It wasn't Crossways. It was Castles, the one nearer the field. But first, they took him to say good-bye to Mrs. Warner.

Prince seemed to know that he was going to a new home and nuzzled up to the old lady to say farewell. His coat shone in the winter sunshine and his eyes twinkled brightly like diamonds.

Mrs. Warner's eyes filled with tears as she gave Prince one last hug.

"We have friends who ride at the stable," said Emma. "And we'll make sure that we come riding this way as often as we can."

"Thank you, my dear," said Mrs. Warner. "At least I can stop worrying about Prince now. It's such a relief to know where he is. And I'll write to Mrs. Lewis and tell her what's happened. I'm sure she meant well. But it's good that you and Sheltie came along when you did!"

"Sheltie has a nose for trouble." Emma laughed.

"Well, it's lucky he has." Mrs. Warner smiled.

Sheltie threw up his head and blew a raspberry. Then he pranced on the spot, eager to get going and deliver his friend to his new home at Castles riding school, a stable fit for a Prince.